garbage
a darker religion

by Mark Freeth

 POP CULTURE

Created by Pop Culture, published by OZone Books, a division of Bobcat
Books, distributed by Book Sales Ltd., Newmarket Road, Bury St. Edmunds,
Suffolk IP33 3YB.

Copyright © 1997 OZone Books

Order No: 02100012
ISBN: 07119.6782.2

The author and publisher have made every effort to contact all copyright
holders. Any, who for whatever reason have not been contacted are invited
to write to the publishers so that so that a full acknowledgement may be
made in subsequent editions of this work

Picture credits: Redferns, All Action, Rex features, Angela Lubrano, Steve
Double.

Design by:

garbage

a darker religion

by Mark Freeth

Contents

A darker religion

1

The curious musical climate that gave rise to Garbage was complicated to say the least. But then, how could it not be, given the many and varied genres riddling the US. For some 40 years now it has been constantly influencing and being influenced by what's been going on musically around the rest of the world - a rich history indeed that includes the very birth of rock'n'roll.   But we need to narrow it down here, define our terms as it were, because we are talking about modern alternative rock. The term 'alternative' poses some difficulty when applied to music these days, given the 'alternatives' to the 'alternative', so to speak, that are increasingly on offer. But I'm sure that all of us here recognise a difference between, say, PJ Harvey and Sonia, or say, Machine Head and Bon Jovi? And need I hold a gun to your head to ascertain which you prefer? No? Fine. That's as good a starting point as any, I guess. But while much 'alternative' music might end up resembling its 'straighter' cousin, and vice versa, it is 'attitude' that makes a true alternative.

However, lest anyone out there gets the impression that we're about to embark on some kind of 'alternative music is ace, whilst all mainstream music is pap' trip - think again. If there's one theme that will be cropping up time and time again throughout this tome, it will be that its subject is about one of a few bands that have managed to appeal - and be successful in - both areas. But, their starting point definitely had its roots in the area we're defining as 'alternative' music.

So bearing this in mind, anyone with even a modest grasp on the who's, why's and wherefore's of the underbelly of the Great Beast we call the Music Business will understand that, although there are no absolutes in popular music, and without wishing to oversimplify matters too much, it's probably fair to say that without the late '60s being set alight by the anarchic, self-destructive psychedelic rock of the Stooges, there would be no musical uprising we know as punk rock. Without punk rock there would have been no slacker shifting down a gear to what we call 'grunge' (more of that in a moment), and without ' grunge' there would have been no Garbage. Probably.

The 'grunge' factor is perhaps the most problematic. The term itself has come to leave a faddish aftertaste in the mouth, and although it was a media

A darker religion

generated 'movement' as was punk, it doesn't seem to have weathered as well as its anti-establishment cousin, which always appeared to have the underlying, energetic, socio-political ideology attached to its art college roots. Whereas 'grunge' quickly became a byword for all that was listless and downbeat, a 'drop out' culture (without the colour of its hippy predecessor) which even the exciting music it aligned itself with couldn't drag it away from.

hat is certain, however, is that Butch Vig's and Steve Marker's Smart Studio (which Vig started to put together at the tail end of the '70s with gear bought from a band called The Shoes. The Shoes's Gary Kebe, incidentally, helped out production-wise on early Spooner recordings - again more of that later), became associated with the 'scene' almost by default. Before 'grunge' even had a name, Smart was recording cutting edge outfits like Killdozer, Tad and Smashing Pumpkins for forward-thinking labels like Sub Pop and Touch & Go. Labels at the forefront of a new 'alternative' American scene that helped change the industry for good. Or ill?. Oh yes, alongside all those who saw the Seattle explosion (it's interesting to note here, that much of the recorded 'sound' behind the scene came out of the Midwest where Smart was based, rather than Seattle where much of the emphasis was later placed, and to where many bands flocked to get a piece of the action) as one of the most liberating American musical events since the West Coast spat out those mighty punk rock pioneers Black Flag and their own SST label in the late '70s, there were some

'purists' who saw it as a 'betrayal' of a whole host of punk ethics. Why? Oh, something to do with the 'underground' believing that an elite army of bands, artists, writers, photographers, etc., had 'sold out' to The Man. Again. Shades of paranoid, punk rock-saturated Britain circa 1977, or what?

Truth is, no one was 'selling out' to anyone. All that was happening was a bunch of garage bands (and yes, a lot of them were from middle-class backgrounds, but since when was 'alternative', 'underground' music the sole property of the working class?) suddenly had the opportunity to introduce their art to a wider cross section of people, and thus open the floodgates into the mainstream. In fact, 'grunge's' impact has meant that it has almost become the norm for rock in the States. The net result of this is a far healthier music scene than ever, with more and more 'out there' bands charting, and a massive cross-pollination of music, whereby you'll find the same kids at hardcore metal gigs as at funky hip-hop jams and all-night raves. And anyone who can find fault with that kind of breakdown of tribal barriers within our culture, may as well stop reading now.

Add a dash of UK post-punk flavouring in the shape of the Scottish take-no-bullshit-from-anyone female singer Shirley Manson, to three guys who came out of this seething US melting pot, and you have Garbage. Before anyone had heard a note or seen a publicity shot, everyone knew that Garbage were going to be Something Special. You only had to hold that first single Vow in your hot little hands, and wonder who in their right minds would package a limited run of 7-inch vinyl records in a metal case (Public Image Limited and their Metal Box aside, of course) hoping it would sell. It had to be someone weird, right? Someone who cared nothing for the trifles of chart success, right? Well, right and wrong.

A darker religion

Certainly, when Vow was placed on turntables back in March '95, there was an obvious 'oddness' to it - a bending of the accepted way pop/rock records should sound. But there was also an embracing of what makes a great pop record : a catchy melody, a rhythm you can dance to and a killer chorus. Sounds a trite recipe doesn't it? But what Garbage added was a dark, menacing 'attitude', an adrenaline-fuelled 'angst' that clearly stated that they were going to have no problems whatsoever in planting a boot firmly in both those mainstream and 'alternative' camps. They were about to change the way a whole bunch of people thought about and made music - from the inside.

No doubt about it, Garbage were indeed continuing that respected musical lineage traceable back to The Stooges (bizarrely, even Manson's pre-Garbage outfit, Goodbye Mr Mackenzie, covered the classic Stooges track I'm Sick of You!) but, as is only right and proper, lacing it with a sharp '90s technological bent. Did someone say dance?! Yep, if there is a latter-day musical genre that is carrying the torch for Punk Rock Attitude, it's the whole dance culture. And like hip-hop before it, its roots lie in a coming together of Art and The Street.

It embraces a DIY code which allows for just about anybody to get involved, even those computer geeks holed up in their bedrooms who haven't even thought about music before. The kids are doing it for themselves again. Once more, they aren't hanging on until they've passed all their music exams before getting out there and doing it. Once more, they aren't begging record companies to sign 'em up - they're simply forming their own labels. So, although house, techno, dance, trance, ambient and all its myriad offshoots are coming from a different musical frame (having said that, it shouldn't come as any surprise that many of todays dance culture movers and shakers cut their teeth on punk rock), the mind frame is the same. Garbage knows this, and have utilised some of dance's rhythmic drive to their own ends. So while a tenuous link can be made between 'grunge' and Garbage (though no doubt the band won't thank you for it!) there's no escaping the fact that they are indeed a new breed of punk rockers.

a stroke of luck

Producer, drummer and fx wizard Butch Vig should need no introduction. But for the uninitiated, when not dragging rock'n'roll round the back of the bike sheds and giving it a damn good thrashing (then snogging it to death), he and guitarist Steve Marker run the aforementioned Smart Studio in very rock'n'roll Madison, Wisconsin and have been since '84. Here in-between recording a multitude of angry, young punk gunslingers, they'd put down their own stuff, thus planting a seed for what was to become one of the most innovative, hard-edged pop sounds of the '90s. Before Garbage came to fruition though, Vig's production name was on everyone's lips as 'the man behind Nirvana.' For the record, Vig didn't actually start working with the 'grunge' kings till March 1990, when the project that became Nevermind began at Smart. Although one might equally argue that he was as much responsible for the sound we know and love behind US art-punk pioneers Sonic Youth (Experimental Jet Set), loud'n'snotty

a stroke of luck

punksters L7 (Bricks Are Heavy), and misfits-made-good, Smashing Pumpkins (Gish, Lull, and Siamese Dream).

Vig, Marker and guitarist Duke Erikson had worked together since the year dot in the nearly-but-not-quite bands Spooner and Firetown, and so it seemed only natural for them to eventually knuckle down and work on a 'serious project' of their own again. In 1993, that project became Garbage - so called after a local musician delivered his verdict on seeing the mess of tape accumulated during some of the early recordings. That local musician was later thanked for his contribution to Garbage history by further contributing to their music himself - Pauli Ryan played percussion on a couple of the tracks of the debut album.

But it wasn't until '94 that the line-up was famously completed, when in a brilliant '90s trash culture, turning-on-its-head, take-on-placing-an-ad-in-the Melody Maker moment, a chance single screening by MTV's 120 Minutes (at 2AM, no less!) of the video to Anglefish's Suffocate Me single, brought singer Shirley Manson to Marker's and the rest of the guys' attention. Rumours abound that Vig also approached Ruby's Lester Rankine and Sonic Youth's Kim Gordon for the post. He strenuously denies the former, whilst has no problem whatsoever admitting the latter. Perfect. 'We needed a singer' he told i-d's Frank Broughton, 'and we wanted a woman. We were pretty set on that.' Vig called her up and asked her to join him and the boys for a session. There then followed a telephone call

from Manson to her record company asking who the hell this guy Vig was! 'I thought he'd be a curly-haired creep, clad in tight leather pants' she told Select's Caspar Smith. 'He's quite the opposite : delicate, with impeccable manners.'

After being told to go check out the small print on the cover of Nevermind , she accepted the opportunity to audition.

'I was in way over my head', Manson admitted to Rolling Stone's Jancee Dunn. 'But the guys were equally as nervous.'

'We didn't know what to do!' recalled Marker to i-d . 'I think she was pretty disgusted at that.'

'To me, Shirley had a darkness and a depth to her that you don't get out of many bands that are around right now', Marker told Volume's Anne Scanlon, 'it really, really struck me the first time I heard her.'

'I think the first thing that struck all four of us', continued Erikson, 'the minute we sat down at the table together, was we knew we could all be friends. Just like that.'

'I met them and fell in love with them', Manson added simply.

It's clear that whatever awkwardness hung in the air during that initial meeting, the all-important chemistry had begun to take effect, and a close bond was all but sealed. Garbage was on the way to becoming a fully-fledged, bone fide band. However, 'We actually didn't set out to have a band', says Marker, 'we were locked in a room with cheap beer

'I met them and fell in love with them'

'I used to read stories about people in bands or movie actresses or models – people who had fallen into lucky, fantastic jobs, and it would piss me off because I'd think "that really doesn't happen", things like that do not happen. And now I realise that something like that happened to me.'

and potato chips and this is what it turned into.' But a band they became, albeit to some pundits, smelling faintly of 'producer supergroup.'

Marker told Guitar's Danny Eccleston : 'I realised that people were going to look at it sceptically at first. But the guys in the band are not the cliched idea of what a record producer is. We don't have Ferraris or blow-dried hair or gold medallions around our necks. We're basically rock band guys that learned how to work in the studio, just as a way to live.' Besides, to offset any suspicion that Garbage was in any way a 'manufactured' outfit, there was the veritable fairy tale aspect of the way Manson became involved. She mused to i-d, 'I used to read stories about people in bands or movie actresses or models - people who had fallen into lucky, fantastic jobs, and it would piss me off because I'd think "that really doesn't happen", things like that do not happen. And now I realise that something like that happened to me.'

Of course, it hadn't always been this way...

3

Alien sex fiends all
Shirley Manson

Offspring of an ex-jazz singer (mum) and lecturer in poultry genetics (!) (dad), 30 year-old Edinburgh born'n'bred Manson's first taste of fame came at 16. 'I lost interest in school', she told Rolling Stone, 'because I discovered rock'n'roll, smoking and drinking.' She began stabbing keys and warbling in the background somewhere with Goodbye Mr Mackenzie, where she obtained solid grounding in the in's and out's of a working band, and had a good ol' time to boot! Apart, that is, from falling prey to one of the unwritten no-no's in bands : Never Go Out With Another Member. 'Watching the man you're in love with', (singer Martin), 'fuck other girls was not a particularly nice thing to live with', she admitted to Rolling Stone, 'it literally broke me.'

Amazing as it may seem, given the supreme con-fidence she now exudes, Manson had always been prone to bouts of self-loathing, which the aforementioned heart-wrenching experience could have only compounded.

'I was a horrible child. I was really vile', she recalled to Melody Maker's Dave Simpson. 'I was convinced I was the ugliest creature that ever lived.' By her own admission, she's 'an absolute neurotic' and 'I have a really horrible temper. If something fucks me off, I just snap. I can't control it.' Which kind of makes you wonder how on earth she manages to survive in the environment she's in, in the frontline of one of the most credible, newsworthy bands of the '90s. Where the possibility of something, somebody, somewhere 'fucking you off' virtually every day is extremely likely. Was there anything positive she felt she was bringing to the team? 'What did I add?' she throws back, 'a bad temper!'

An old school chum remembers a very different

'I want a man who will let me

ee in his bellybutton.'

Shirley Manson

Shirley Manson. Someone who was confident and at ease with herself, someone who was having fun and about to take exactly what she wanted from life, but gladly offering something in return.

'I went to high school with Shirley' she says, 'so I knew her from about 12 to 17. We were fairly close up to around the break-up of Goodbye Mr Mackenzie, but I haven't spoken to her for years. The school was in Stockbridge - a fairly Bohemian part of Edinburgh, and it concentrated a lot on art, drama and music. Shirley started off as a dancer, then got very involved in drama and was very much part of an "arty" scene. One or two of her friends from that time also became fairly famous themselves in the entertainment industry, including Chris Connelly (Ministry, Revolting Cocks), who was really a close friend (to the extent that Connelly name-checks Manson on the sleeve notes to his album Phenobrb Bambalam)

'So there was a group of about three or four girls who were incredibly pretty and talented , and she was one of those. But Shirley always had a bit of an edge to her - she was always at parties and she was quite often drunk! She definitely had what you might call 'star quality' and charisma. Anyway, I didn't see her for a few years, but she was really good friends with an ex-boyfriend of mine, and she was very much a face round Edinburgh - everyone knew her. She was always good fun, with a great sense of humour - very lavatorial, she never did anything outrageous, despite always being the centre of attention.'

And an equally positive summing up of Manson's qualities perhaps inevitably comes from one of the boys in the band. Vig describes her as : 'Sometimes scary, sometimes dreamy, sometimes sexy, sometimes psychotic. What more could you ask for?'

Which elicits the kind of telling response from Manson we were waiting for : 'It makes me feel good when someone says I sing my heart out. That's what music's about - freedom..'

Ten 'interesting revelations from Manson's own mouth

(as told to Details and Rolling Stone)

'I'm sick of tattoos, sick of piercing, sick of temporary tattoos. They are the white stillettoes of the '90s.'

'I'm glad I don't have a big black bush!'

'I love it when I pull down a boy's pants and he's got no knickers on.'

'I want a man who will let me pee in his bellybutton.'

'There's a pitiful flaw in my personality that subconsciously makes me want to do the exact opposite of what's expected of me.'

'I used to go out with this boy who would not and could not perform oral sex. Clearly he wasn't a real man.'

'I can't stand someone who can outdepress me.'

revelations from Manson's own mouth

'Spontaneous sex in spontaneous places...helps keep the fire alive.'

'You could see my arse. And if that wasn't humiliation enough, this boy in the audience who had a personal grudge against me, told the whole world that I had a huge big pair of granny pants on. I have never worn granny pants! In fact, I didn't have any pants on!' (On realising half way through a Goodbye Mr Mackenzie gig, that she'd tucked her shirt into her tights.)

'My man has to be cool enough to say, "What did you do today, darling?" and hear me reply, "Well, I put my crotch next to Gavin Rossdale's for the cover of Details", and not blink an eye. It takes a strong man to love a famous woman.'

3

Butch Vig

Next to Manson, Vig is probably the other individual name that most people associate with Garbage. Although, in the beginning when Vow proudly presented itself to the world, even Manson had to admit that one of the main reasons so many people were interested in them was because of Vig's involvement. 'I doubt if we'd had got the same degree of attention if it wasn't for Butch Vig's Nirvana connection', she admitted to the NME's Amy Raphael after only two singles had been released. 'Until people have the music at their fingertips, it's the only newsworthy thing. People will want to listen to us because he's involved, or they'll totally disregard it for the same reason.'

Talking to Feature's Mike Gee, Vig said, 'It's funny, there I was in the beginning - Butch Vig, cool producer of Nirvana and The Pumpkins. Everyone wanted to talk to me, all the focus was on me. A year later it's like "Butch who? Oh you mean the drummer in the Shirley Manson band."'

The 'Nirvana connection' is one of the things that Vig is forever going to feel proud of and rue the day it ever happened. When talking to him, predictably and understandably, people are always going to want to bring up the subject of Kurt Cobain and his suicide in 1994. Equally predictably and equally understandably, Vig is reluctant to be pressed on the matter, having formed a close working relationship with the 'tortured artist' and so-called 'spokesman' for a generation. He remembered in front of Melody Maker, 'That was just so terrible...I still get so...despondent, that Kurt felt so awful he couldn't go on living anymore. I hear the stuff on the radio and it just gives me a chill to hear his voice.'

Which is as good a reason as any to draw a respectful veil over the subject. One might argue, that at 40, grown men ought not to be embarking on a career as a rock'n'roll star - they should be thinking of settling down with the family. Or, if they insist on sticking with the music biz, then at least have the dignity to get behind the scenes, f' god's sake. Trust the retiring (?) (you never know in this business), Wisconsinian (dairy farming community of Viroqua to be exact), 'alternative rock guru' Butch Vig to go the other way around.

But then Vig was a maverick from the start. Son of a music teacher mother and doctor father, his childhood heroes were The Who, who he first witnessed on a Smothers Brothers TV show, and it was they who inspired him to ditch the piano lessons, get his first drum kit and join his first band, The Schlichts (named after the singer Kevin Schlicht). Various other college combos followed, leading him to hook up with Steve and Duke in 1983, resulting in him dropping out of Madison's University of Wisconsin (where he studied film, and where he became interested in movie soundtracks and thus synthesised the sounds and special effects which pervade Garbage's material today) to concentrate on Spooner, and afterwards, Firetown.

A year later, Vig and Marker founded Smart and it wasn't long before they, along with Erikson, found themselves three of

'I don't wanna be a rock'n'roll sta

Butch Vig

the most sought after producers and remixers (for the likes of Depeche Mode, Nine Inch Nails, House of Pain and U2 - some CV, eh?) in the business. Vig stepped further into the limelight of course, with his work on Nirvana and The Pumpkins. Then came Garbage, and Vig saw the opportunity to come from behind the desk and go back on the road - Big Time. Well, who wouldn't?

Vig marvelled to Feature , 'I spend years living in studios, in one place for months on end, then suddenly I'm living from town to town, hotel to hotel, endlessly. I think we'll be glad when we finally say "stop, that's enough". I don't think you realise how much you actually miss people until you get back and actually see them when you're in a comfortable place again.'

Catching Vig in just such a comfortable place a few days before the release of Stupid Girl, and therefore a rare calm moment before the storming success of the said single, I asked him why he thinks that Garbage seems to appeal to such a wide cross section of people. Shrugging he says, 'I really don't know, I guess we're just lucky in that we decided to make a pop record. But we brought to it a kind of darkness. I think we thought we'd get more criticism from the 'indie' press because I was involved, but we now feel more like a band, which I think had more to do with the process of making the album. But yeah, it's amazing that people have responded really favourably to it.'

I continued , 'The pressure must have been on though, given your involvement with Nirvana. Has the connection ever caused any problems?'

'I think once people heard the music, they didn't give a shit', he replied. 'I'm sure that if we'd've really sucked, we'd've been a bigger target for the press. Again, I think we're lucky in that we started in America, where people listen to more styles of music, whereas general-ly speaking, people here tend to stick with one category.'

But whatever people are into over here, most of them seem to get off on Garbage, as evidenced by the record sales and the turn out for their live performances. And what live performances! Later, we'll be looking in detail at just how Garbage transfer to the fleshy arena, but it was a timely moment to ask Vig if it proved problematic in any way, attempting to replicate live the album's uniquely clinical edge.

Butch admits, 'Initially, we were pretty intimidated by how we were gonna reproduce the record live. But what we did was strip the songs down to their core elements, and then start rearranging the structures, keys, etc., add the samples and stuff, and it worked out pretty good.' Despite Butch's earlier claim that Garbage simply set out to make a 'pop' record, there is evidently something 'else' attached to this particular 'pop' band, something, well 'strange' for want of a better word. Does Butch think it is important these days for even our pop stars (as opposed to our supposedly terminally 'weird' rock stars) to be 'out there?'

'It just doesn't work if a pop or rock star tries to be weird', Butch answers. 'It's to do with a certain chemistry within someone that makes them the way they are. Certainly, a lot of people we know seem to be very 'odd' indeed, and most of them appear to hail from little isolated Midwestern towns, were people can feel very lost and can end up going mad. I think you'll find a lot of our serial killers come from places like that.'

Which echoes an earlier comment from Manson, 'I find the most normal people full of excess and rebellion. Weirdness lurks in the most unlikely corners.'

'But in terms of us', Vig continues, 'yeah there's obviously a tendency for Shirley's lyrics to be morose, but we all have some fun with it, that's very important - for the rock generation to be able to make fun of themselves. Anyway, I like the idea of having these really dark lyrics next to a shiny pop melody!'

The best of both worlds, as it were. And the result being, of course, a wonderfully perverse form of entertainment gnawing away at our safe, precious social mores...

Ten 'interesting revelations' from Vig's own mouth

(as told to Goldmine, the NME, Melody Maker and Volume)

'I think I'm very average. As much as I love Keith Moon, I couldn't play like that.' (On Vig's prowess on the drums).

'I'm just the fucking drummer, man! I drum! I just wanna sit back and drink some beers and rock out.'

'I'm a total pop geek! Vig admits, citing Glen Campbell's Witchita Lineman as the perfect example of a pop song.

'Grunge died before it was even really born - may it rest in peace.'

'We love Madison. It's good to have a place to go where there's no bullshit. People will call you on it if you act pretentious.'

'Shirley is very feisty - she's got a mean right hook. When she gets pissed off, she goes, "fuck you, you deserve a dead arm!" So both my arms are black and blue. Duke and Steve are the same, we're all bruised up!'

'I'm very proficient on kazoo!'

'I don't wanna be a rock'n'roll star.'
'My name always confuses people - I've had a couple of Bruces over the past few days. I recently received a parcel addressed to "Mr Butch Big", and when we were doing press in Germany, the journalists kept asking, really earnestly, "Botch Wig, what is the essence of Garbage?"'

'I'll go for the broody, self-destructive, self-loathing, alcoholic drug addict.' (On the possibilities that fame has to offer).

3

Duke Erikson

(as told to Vox, Rolling Stone, i-d,
Details, the NME, Guitar and Melody
Maker)

'I feel like a star', said Duke during
Garbage's first UK press conference.

'Like, so we only play one gig a
week? Sounds good to me!' (On the
idea of arriving in countries a few
days early to take in some sights).

'At one point, we were working in
the studio and had forgotten what we
were doing. All of a sudden I go
'Where's Shirley?' I went upstairs,
and she's sitting on the floor, looking
out of the window, petting the cat'.
(On Manson's audition).

'I studied art at a tiny college in
Nebraska, and I taught drawing there
a couple of semesters...' (pause) '...is
this really interesting to anybody?'

What were we saying about grown men? Hell,
Erikson (distant relation to 13th Floor
Elevator, Roky Erikson. Wouldn't you just kill
for that kind of cool musical pedigree?) is 45!
But what does age matter in the Peter Pan
world of rock'n'roll? Sure, there's nothing
worse than seeing some tired, withered ol'
rocker still trying to out-strut his or her
teenage contemporaries, but what about the experience an older
musician can bring to an outfit? Someone who can lend , how shall
we say, a dignified presence to the line-up? Take a bow Duke (Doug
to his mates). That said, he, along with Vig and Marker, weren't too
old to be later rounded up by Shirley, load up on Ecstasy and truck
on down to a techno club for the first time in their lives...

But apart from the odd detour into the pits of rock'n'roll
excess, that's calm, intense, dry-humoured, Nebraskan Duke
Erikson for you. He's been at it since he was 16, the first band being
The British (!) (Gig posters would read 'The British are coming!...uh
oh...). He also studied art and paid the rent via many a stop-gap job
(truck driving, carpentry...) in-between. Like Vig and Marker, Erikson
eventually turned his hand to production, until the call of The Wild
gave him the opportunity to sell his soul to ol'Nick one more time.
Clearly Erikson has no shame.

'I feel like a star'

revelations from Erikson's own mouth

'I felt like I had known her in another life.' (On meeting Manson for the first time).

'I've never had this much fun before : this is me having fun.'

'Things can get a little dull in the studio when there's no one but boys there - you need a little romance to get you through the day.' (On reading Carla Simpson's Seductive Caress).

'They're either too big or too small. You know how it is.' (On condoms).

'Steve can play the lead line from Siberian Khatru by Yes, and I can't.

'We gladly allow the queen to rule.' (On Manson being the centre of attention).

3

Steve Marker

'The scary, psychotic one', as described by Shirley. 37-year-old Marker went to high school in Mamroneck, just outside New York City. He met Butch and Duke at the University of Wisconsin, whilst studying communication arts. He played in a band called The Flying Saucers and First Person with Vig, and acted as a roadie for Spooner. He went into partnership with Butch to set up Smart (in fact, it was Steve's early experiments with 4-track equipment that inspired the two to set up a full-blown recording studio), and is now back rocking it out in the same band as Vig after all these years. Funny how things come around...

'I thought Roxy Music came from Mars.'

Daniel Schulman and Mike Kashou

Who're they? You might well ask. Daniel Schulman and Mike Kashou are the 'fifth and sixth Beatles', the extra pieces of Garbage if you will. They're bassmen and are called on to help out when the band go out on the road and into the studio respectively. Respect due. (Although there have no doubt been 'interesting revelations' from Daniel and Mike's own mouths, none have yet to be recorded for posterity. We wait with baited breath...)

Ten 'interesting revelations' from Marker's own mouth

(as told to Vox, Rolling Stone, Melody Maker, Addicted To Noise, and Retroactive Baggage)

'It was very inspirational for our first show.' (Upon witnessing GWAR 'decapitate' Jerry Garcia...).

'A lot of bands don't get the chance to be pelted with snowballs while they're playing.' (On performing at America's 'Snoasis' event).

'Now and then a guitar magazine calls you up and asks you what kind of strings you use and that kind of stuff. It's pretty weird. I don't think talking about ourselves comes naturally.'

'I thought she was really nice, but I was very scared of her.' (On meeting Shirley for the first time).

'I thought Roxy Music came from Mars. We've got this video of their early Top of The Pops with Eno in his peacock feathers. I can't believe they didn't all get beat up'

revelations from Marker's own mouth

'Garbage Road Wisdom : if at all possible, try to avoid mid-afternoon concerts on ski hills in New Jersey in sub-zero weather.'

'Garbage Road Wisdom : if at all possible, try to avoid parties with themes that somehow involve tequila, if you have anything at all scheduled during the next two weeks. Like for example, riding in an overcrowded tour bus for an average of ten hours a day, and making really loud noises with electronic instruments while really bright lights flash off and on around you, and people throw shoes at you.'

On playing with one band called the New Upsetters : 'We only knew one song - Pink Floyd's Intersteller Overdrive.'

'I'm studying karate. The next record's going to be mine.(On the 'power struggle' within Garbage.

'We're pretty neurotic about making music.'

4

'I only listen to the sad, sad, songs...'

arbage's sound is one borne out of experiments with hi-tech digital recording gear and techniques, and a return to a basic approach using ancient equipment and analogue systems. Chance also played, and still plays, a key role in creating that warm, yet disturbing sound, from accidental wiring to the random grunting and groaning of instruments in their death throes. 'But whatever weird sounds there are, they have to serve the song', emphathises Erikson.

'Nothing's sacred', Butch agrees, 'the day after pouring your guts into recording, you have to be able to say "erase it". In the end, they're just magnetic impulses.'

'We're trying to make pop music that hopefully doesn't sound like anything else', offered Marker to Melody Maker's Dave Simpson. 'It grew out of the studio work, definitely. Then we began talking about doing this album together, and it would have been kind of dull without vocals, so we needed a singer. And we wanted a woman. We were pretty set on that.'

'I only listen to the sad, sad, songs...'

'We fell in love with her voice', swooned Vig to i-d.

'It was a voice you could remember', Marker continued, 'it felt like there was a connection with the kind of music that we were doing.'

'Shirley gave more edge to some songs than we thought they had', Vig told Addicted To Noise. 'Or she sang them so understated, that she made them more subversive and intense.'

Before Manson got on board, Vig, Marker and Erikson were searching for a sound that Vig describes as, 'Way more fucked-up and experimental. More hardcore than Nine Inch Nails, more rhythmically groovy than a hip-hop record, more guitars than My Bloody Valentine...Once Shirley came in and started singing them and writing lyrics, the songs went more in the direction that we think is better for a pop song.' In other words, Garbage had their cake and were able to eat it - a hard, razor sharp rock sound that would guarantee them 'alternative' credibility, and pop sensibility that would eventually assure them a place in the charts.

'We like a challenge', Marker explained to Guitar, 'and we like new sounds, and it seems to me that since the mid-80s, maybe no one's really exploited what's out there. Rock music and guitar music hasn't taken up the challenge of rap bands like Public Enemy and still retained its character, and yet there's such a lot you can do with samples without going out and buying pristine sample library material. Sample your mistakes and make a song out of it - we've certainly done that.'

'We didn't want to be afraid of using technology', Erikson added, 'but we didn't want to loose the human feel to it either, and we insisted on incorporating classic raw guitar sounds. There are some guitars here and there that don't sound like guitars at all, that sound more like keyboards, so we pushed the envelope a bit there, but we're huge guitar fans. Like, I remember when I was recording the basic guitar track for Vow, and I could not tell you what was plugged into what. But the feedback was amazing. It almost sounded like voices.'

'There are no rules', explains Vig, 'but if the chance is to do less or to do more, usually the answer is more.'

'We let it go as far as we can', adds Erikson, 'then, out of the racket, we pick what we like.'

'It's natural selection applied to chaos', continues Marker, 'the strong overpowers the weak. But when it sounds too clean, we mess it up.' Add to that something...despondent, a morose edge that was sure to keep people guessing.

'Our common ground was a certain melancholy and interest in the perverse', claims Manson. 'It's easy to be morose and hard to be happy. But by the end of recording, I felt we might do something totally la-de-dah. We never did. Maybe the next album will be more jolly.'

Let's hope not.

Garbage's sound can also be detected away from their records, namely in the remixing jobs Vig, Marker and Erikson have done for the likes of the previously mentioned U2, Nine Inch Nails, Depeche Mode and House of Pain. But the band have also invited a string of dance king-pins to mess around with their material, including Rabbit In The Moon, Massive Attack, Goldie and Tricky. Tricky's remixes of the Milk single are worthy of particular

'I only listen to the sad, sad, songs...'

note. Known for his own distinctive, dark, oppressive slant on life, the universe and everything, he was perhaps a perfect choice to work on a Garbage track - especially one so downbeat as Milk. No surprise then that this shadowy collaboration was favourably received by the band, critics and fans alike.

On working with Tricky, Vig told NME, 'We thought he was going to be really introverted and quiet, but he turned out to be the complete opposite. He's really gregarious with a wicked sense of humour and he's a party animal. We went out and got trashed till 6AM in New York and decided we should do some work together. So he flew into Chicago a couple of days later when we had a day off.'

Tricky remembers, 'Garbage wrote Milk and it's a fucking brilliant song, but I just totally stripped it. It was quite a weird session 'cos they were there. And it was quite tense. They weren't into it at first 'cos I work backwards...but after they heard what I was trying to do, they were cool.'

As for possible future collaborators , Steve Marker came up with a particularly original idea for Retroactive Baggage's Tim Simey. 'I'd like to get in someone who doesn't even do remixes - like David Lynch!'

Now, that would be something...

FIRST AID

► 2 A   3   ILFORD HP5 PLUS   ► 3 A   4   ► 4 A   5   ILFORD HP5 P

FIRST AID   FIRST AID

RD HP5 PLUS   ► 8 A   9   7 8 5 6   ► 9 A   10   ILFORD HP5 PLUS   ► 10 A   11

FIRST AID

► 14 A   15   ILFORD HP5 PLUS   15 A   16   7 8 5 6   ► 16 A   17   ILF

FIRST AID

Torn apa

Vow

'The idea for it came from a newspaper article that I read about a woman who had gone back to get revenge on an abusive husband', Butch told Volume about the origins of Vow. 'So we thought it would be cool to get a bit of retribution in there.'

Not actually intended to be Garbage's official debut release, Vow was submitted for inclusion on a compilation with an issue of Volume 1. It was fantastically received, and so it was decided it should be used to introduce the world to Garbage properly, clad in protective armour. Just in case...

And what a little punker it is too! Reminding you that it still wasn't safe to wander alone around Pop Town, not with beasts like this hanging out on street corners...And when we get to that chorus, it does just that in a superb frenzy of punk nihilism, but with the addition of a jewel of a hook that remains welded to your memory banks after only the first listen. But just in case you start getting a little nervous, The End is in sight, gently chiming, floating in to lead the beast out by the hand.

Torn apart

Subhuman

The rubber sleeve, in a way, resonates the song's sensual but disturbing theme. It's an oppressive, industrial, uncompromising workout, but with an occasional glimpse of a 'sweet' 'ooh-ho, ah-ah-ah-ah-ah.'

Only Happy When It Rains

'A song about wanting love, but knowing that life will always get in the way, and of somehow knowing that, and yet not being obliterated by it. It's a song for people that know what it's like to live on the dark side. It's about devotion, but a different kind. A devotion to truth and freedom and to hell with the consequences'

(Shirley Manson)

The ultra-depressive moodiness of the song's subject matter apart, there's an obvious tongue-in-cheek quality lurking behind these darkest, but ultimately satisfying sin-galong melodies. 'We're poking fun at the alternarock angst', Marker explains to Addicted To Noise, 'the wearing your heart on your sleeve thing and poking fun at ourselves for writing such dark songs.'

Queer

'With Queer , I was reading this novel about this woman who was hired to go and make this guy's son "a man". The kid is missing a few marbles. But then he realises that the woman who came to his room is also fucking his father'

(Butch Vig)

Dirty, sexy, dark, infectious with the simplest, but coolest of guitar refrains, copied by Manson's 'do-do-do-do-do-do...', and a bizarre, cabaret-esque, circus-like break, Queer is a seething, throbbing siren, beckoning and enticing.

Stupid Girl

It begins with a sample of The Clash's Train in Vain (which marks it as a Track With Good Taste from the outset) drum intro easing us into the darkest of the dark. There's a hunched, seedy quality to this, that's quite chilling, but with the added warmth that it comes with yet another dream of a chorus. Class, pedigree, sex, raw power, pop power - Stupid Girl has it all.

Milk

Totally different from all the other singles in its gentleness, but still sporting that trademark air of despair, accompanied by a sense of isolation. But true to form, there's also that simple-but-effective Garbage chorus, along with the haunting, ice-blue melody and Manson displaying her aching longing...As such, Milk makes for a fine closure to a fine album. Which, singles aside, leads us neatly into taking a more detailed look at said elpee...

'This is no pop record

singles, album & live reviews

Garbage

'This is no pop record', Vig told Addicted To Noise. 'And while the three of us are too old to be pop stars - we're no Boyz II Men, certainly not teen idols - I think we have made a really good record. If nothing else, the name is fitting. Garbage. Here today, gone tomorrow, but really I hope it's more than that. I hope it's not that disposable. Of course, we have certainly left ourselves open for the ultimate one word record review. "Garbage - indeed!"

So, Garbage were underway, gleaning praise from all quarters, moving closer and closer to that all-important debut album that either establishes you as Serious Contenders, or banishes you to the hell of where-are-they-now? Plus, they had another 'problem' that put extra, undue and unfair pressure on them from the start. Were Garbage at all worried that they were going to attract the wrong kind of attention, with Nirvana's Nevermind meister Butch Vig at the helm? That this debut album was gonna be some kind of 'grunge' all-grown-up affair? Well sort of...

'We knew we had to make a good album...' Manson recalled to Retroactive Baggage. 'If we'd come out with a below-average album, we'd have been crucified...we were shitting ourselves making it!'

Bless 'em. But they knew what they had, and although as individuals and as a band, they couldn't possibly ignore

the impact Nirvana and the whole Seattle scene had upon '90s music - indeed culture - Garbage the album and band, were a different can of worms entirely. So, whilst the sharp, pregnant silences in opener Supervixen only mildly remind us of something similar in Smells Like Teen Spirit, we can say without fear of contradiction or reprisals, that the only aspect that Vig had bought to Garbage which might connect with Nirvana, is an unmistakable 'fuck you!' punk rock attitude. And, of course, a trademark innovative production hand.

But coupled with this smouldering cauldron of resentment and heavy air of menace, is Garbage's distinct attention to melody (albeit dark) and, dare we say it, danceability! Yep, fair to say that you can singalong and dance to every melancholic tale of woe and bitterness, which is what makes it such a wet dream of a 'pop' (albeit heavy - Garbage enjoy 'infecting', don't they?) album, and also what makes each and every one of those tracks a goddamn hit single!

From the aforementioned Supervixen - probably the best opening to an album I've heard in a long time, with that heart-stopping riff having the rug pulled from beneath its boots, as a gentle, lilting refrain takes over, before said riff punches its lights out and drags the thing home. To the agonisingly tearful closer Milk, what we have here, like The Stooges' first, the Sex Pistols' Never Mind The Bollocks, and Jane's Addiction's Nothing Shocking before it , is a monster of a debut album. Vig's drumming is lashed to a beat box throughout, creating a relentless, hypnotic atmosphere, in which Marker's and Erikson's guitars establish mean, sexy grooves and where Manson weaves an evocative series of vocal threads. The subtlety with which she manages this,

evokes a sensuality that strokes the flesh, while the guys' industrial raging puts the fear of God up you - just check As Heaven Is Wide if you don't believe me...

'1,2,3...' whispers Manson before 'Not My Idea' stutters into hearing range, and lurches drunkenly and rhythmically through its chorus, scarily juxtaposed with her nursery rhyme-like 'duh, duh, duh, duh, duh, duh, duhhh...' A Stroke Of Luck wanders through a dense forest, where unnerving, moving shadows are always at the edge of your vision. Dog New Tricks contains a killer punky guitar break where Manson gets all Iggy Pop-like on our asses. My Lover's Box's dense gothic intro makes way for a subdued, creeping verse and epic chorus with Manson's sorrowful plea. Fix Me Now's hip-hoppy intro and Manson's PJ Harvey-like gasping, gives way to one of the dirtiest, grooviest guitar riffs you'll have heard in a long time, and once again, the chorus ensures you'll be singing it all the way to your lover's arms...

Garbage's lyrics (despite Manson being the vehicle for their expression, are in fact a group effort. However, the handwriting on the sleeve notes are all her own work - fact fans!), contain elements of hate, sorrow, self-deprecation, loathing, sulkiness and sultriness. Although, it would be a mistake to assume that Manson is baring her and her boys' deepest, innermost thoughts.

It's all too easy to believe a songwriter's lyrics come from the heart : '...the songs are a lot like acting', Vig told Retroactive Baggage, 'you have to really get into the part. It shouldn't be taken too literally...' However, it's probably safe to say that one or two of the sentiments contained in the words are borne out of Manson's anger, bitterness or regret. 'I speak before I think', she admitted. 'I always hurt people inadvertently.'

But she is sussed enough to acknowledge that she's not the only member of the outfit. 'Because there are two sexes in the band, there are certain things that wouldn't be appropriate maybe', Manson explained to Addicted To Noise. 'Or that I would want to sing about, but that the boys' didn't really give a rat's ass about. I'd want to sing about my periods, but I don't think the boys would be particularly interested in working all day in the studio on that kind of thing. We try to find a common ground.'

'You'd love to sing about your periods?' quizzed Erikson mockingly.

'When we started writing lyrics', Vig explained to Volume about Garbage's pre-Manson months, 'we tried to write a lot of them from a woman's perspective, and I think, initially, some of them were a little pretentious. But as soon as Shirley came on board, she simplified the lyrics so that they were a lot more subtle and worked better as songs.'

Conversely, Manson appears not to have any difficulty in getting behind the male psyche : 'I've been accused by male friends of thinking like a man', she says, 'maybe it comes from being small-chested!'

As for specifics, lyrically speaking, Garbage prefer to leave little to the imagination. 'We felt that we didn't want any of the songs to be exclusive to one person', Shirley pointed out to Raw's Cathi Unsworth. 'We wanted a lot of people to relate to them. I'm always disappointed when you listen to songs and then you hear the band explain what they mean, and what you thought about it was the complete opposite of what it really meant.'

So, room enough to bring our own personal baggage to what amounts to a piece of work that runs the whole gamut of human emotions - particularly the darker ones. 'We make a cool record', Vig readily admitted to Record Collector. 'But I don't think we really are cool. Maybe Shirley is, but we are a bunch of geeks.' The day before the album came out, Butch Vig was heard to say to Addicted To Noise, 'I guess after tomorrow we'll know if we even need to do anymore interviews.'

And finally, as if to put the last nail in Garbage's creation once and for all, Vig maddeningly described the album as, 'A record for pop geeks who dance with the lights out.' There's that word again. That makes about three million of us 'geeks', and counting...

At the time of writing, March/April 1997, Garbage are hunkered down at Smart, recording the second album for an end of '97/early '98 release. 'There's a lot riding on the next album for all of us', Vig admitted to Feature's Mike Gee, 'so we'll probably all have nervous breakdowns recording it...'

But what of Garbage live? How does the awesome power of the recorded works transfer to the stage? It was a question in the back of the minds of anyone who'd yet to have their cherry deftly plucked by these grim popsters. Looking back at my notes from just such an occasion, even I had my doubts...

Civic Hall, Wolverhampton, UK
(March 19, 1996)

There's a feeling of trepidation in the air for those of us who are seeing Garbage live for the first time, and there's a nervous biting of nails. After all, you don't live for nearly six months with probably one of the most near-perfect 'alternative' pop/rock albums in a long time and not wonder, 'how the hell are they gonna pull that off live?' Especially when that album has never once tried to disguise its inventive use of loops, samples and a whole host of mind-boggling recording technology.

It seems like a lot of people tonight are wondering the same thing, the hall is rammed and a few casual enquiries reveal that, like me, there's no shortage of virgins to the live Garbage experience. And what a First Time it turns out to be!

Sold out virtually as soon as it went on sale, here are Garbage in a mid-range venue on the first date of this UK tour, in a bigger league than on previous visits, and as such, I can't help feeling a sense of disappointment as the band take another step just out of reach. Inevitably, we all get ridiculously precious about our bands, jealously guarding them from too many fans, or from too much fame, whilst reacting incredulously to those who don't share our passion. I'm positioned over halfway back, lost amongst the throng, and I'm thinking, 'I'm not gonna like this.' But goddammit, Garbage just ups and explodes right in our faces, filling that sprawling stage with blistering white light, heat and sound, and showering the hall with a kind of exotic shrapnel that makes even us out here in the sticks feel like we're mere inches away from our Heroes For The Night.

Manson prowls the boards, spitting out her Tales Of The Weird , whilst Butch and the boys cast a discreet veil here and expose a slimy underbelly there. We either bounce around like mad fools, or, at the end, shake ourselves to our senses, pick our jaws up from the floor realising we've just lost an hour or so of real time, and stumble out of the hall wondering what the hell happened back there...

In fact, what happened was, in one way or another, everyone present participated in a strange event which could only loosely be termed as a 'rock gig', steered by artistes who suffer a disservice by being called a 'band'. There was a whole 'other' thing going on - something very dark, but very sensual. Yeah, that was certainly 'something else...' Garbage did indeed Rule The World.

So there it was - proof, if proof were needed, that Garbage could do no wrong on record or live. But just to make sure, how about the opportunity to catch them in a cosier venue? Seems like there is a God after all...

Metropolitan University
Radio 1 Sound city live broadcast,
Leeds, UK (April 9, 1996)

I'm working on this gig, and as such I have an enviable but distorted vantage point from the photo-pit, stage left. I have to tell you - I'm in awe. And I feel slightly guilty because of it. Sure, there's Garbage - a whole band, confident, playing their guts out, working that stage...but I can't take my eyes off Manson. I watch her in relatively close-up profile throughout the gig, and I witness a slender woman transform herself into some kind of demonic creature that's scary and sexy at the same time. And genuinely riveting. She also transforms the nail-biting audience into a wild-eyed beast, unable to contain itself any longer - the place goes apeshit!

I catch myself staring open-mouthed and shift my gaze to the front row, where a knot of grubby adolescents are trying to look up Manson's mini-skirt. This angers me, but it's tempered by my aforementioned guilt-attack, stemming from what amounted to drooling voyeurism. Seems like none of us are innocent - I've even spoken to women who cite Manson (among other female performers) as a sexual fantasy figure. So, I turn my attention to the back of the stage to study, in a more serious manner, the band that is Garbage. I discover a unit skin tight, born out of hard graft and experience, with the application of some of the technology used on the album, which, far from too closely clinically replicating its sound or sanitising the live vibe, positively adds to the mood, injecting an unmistakable chilling 'edge' to yer regular night out to 'catch a band.'

It's all over far too quickly. The nature of the event (shortened sets to cram in three bands between 6 and 10PM to go out live on the air), means we feel cheated and satiated all at the same time. In fact, a state of minor confusion seems par for the course in Garbage's world. Emotions are jangled by their evocative sights and sounds, and I walk from the show and back to my hotel shunning company, in an indescribably 'altered state'.

'What we're doing is entertainment', Manson explained to Rolling Stone about what they do. 'When you go out and gig, it's not some fucking cathartic intellectual exercise, it's base entertainment.'

Supervixen

Although any Woman In Rock worth her salt would rather be judged on her art, than the fact she's 'a woman', you have to admire any woman entering the male-dominated arena that is the music business. Here, people make up their mind about you the moment you step onto that stage or in front of that camera.. It's getting easier though, with so many more women behind the scenes, and so many more powerful role models coming to the fore.

Skunk Anansie's Skin, Alanis Morrisette, Angel Cage's Jean Hare, Portishead's Beth Gibbons, Ruby's Lesley Rankine, Bjork, PJ Harvey ('I think she's unbelievably amazing', Manson told Raw, 'I just adore her records and I play them all the time. I think she's seriously underrated. I heard her on some radio show the other night and she's got a really beautiful, soft, calm voice'), Naomi, Patti Rothberg, Courtney Love ('I'm a huge admirer', Manson also admitted to Feminism Amplified's Kim France, 'she's vulnerable and I warm to that. She's incredibly intelligent and incredibly articulate and she's not afraid to open her mouth and attack anybody or anything. She's neither black nor white and that's why I think she irritates a lot of people. But that's what I find endearing about her'). To name but a few.

And a whole host of older gals to use as a starting point : Betty Davis, Janis Joplin, Neneh Cherry, Patti Smith, Debbie Harry, Siouxsie Sioux, Chrissie Hynde, etc. - the 'scary women of pop?' Not according to Shirley Manson, 'I don't think there's anything scary about them', she reckoned to Retroactive Baggage , 'I just think they're striking, they're individualists, and that upsets people at times.

It frightens people because society in general makes us think we're not supposed to be like that. They're strong women, and that intimidates men.'

We can certainly count Manson among the aforementioned list. With Garbage gigs fairly evenly balanced between guys 'n gals, it's perhaps safe to assume that it won't be long before we'll be witnessing a shed load more of Women In Rock. Inevitably, once you have a woman fronting a band, there's the possibility of the 'wrong' kind of attention being levelled at the outfit. One might hazard a guess why some of the guys are fascinated by Manson, but the girls?

'I'm not sure why I get that reaction', mused the object of their attention to Select's Gina Morris. 'Maybe it's because I'm very forthright, not very flirtatious. I'm not a boy-toy. I don't look for approval in men, and I think that's what women find attractive about me. And also because I embrace femininity, I'm not trying to be tough or trying to be this helpless little girl. I can just cope in this male-dominate world without beating my balls.'

'I think the girls come because they want to be like Shirley', Vig reckoned to Feature's Mike Gee. 'They see a lot of power in her performance, just the way she handles herself.' Also in Manson, they maybe also recognise themselves using their sexuality, their femininity in a positive way. There's nothing demeaning about this - after all, it's the woman who's wielding the power here. It's usually the guys who have a problem with it. As Neneh Cherry recently told Brum Beat's Max, 'I haven't got a problem with...I wouldn't exactly call it "exploiting my sexuality", but letting an "air of sensuality" exist. But y'know, it's always there - take a few more items of clothes off, sell a few more records!'

However, 'You have to be careful', Manson warned Arena's Sean Langan. 'The tendency in this business is to make you look beautiful and perfect, but also submissive. And I don't want to be like that.'

'She has something in her that a lot of people don't really have', Vig marvelled to Feature. 'I don't know whether it's star quality, charisma, whatever, but she's got something that when the music goes through her and she's singing it...she's incredibly subtle. She doesn't come across as trying to be heavy handed.'

'People think I've created this image to sell records', Shirley complained to Melody Maker. 'It's me. I'm not weaving a myth, because to me the music is the fantasy. A boy shouted out to me in a concert the other day, "I love you! I love your media created image." I found it really bizarre. I began to think, "Am I pretending to be something I'm not?" But I'm not. It's just the way I am.'

The temptation is, of course, to dwell longer than is absolutely necessary on the fact that Garbage is fronted by a woman, simply because female musicians and female-fronted bands are still in the minority. In these PC times, we should be admiring Garbage for their art, ignoring the fact that their central figure is a woman. To do this is to deny the individual power and distinctive femininity that Shirley Manson - and only Shirley Manson - brings to Garbage.

Funny ol' world, ain't it?...

'I don't look for approval in men, and I think that's what women find attractive about me

Supervixen
Supervixen
Supervixen
Supervixen

As heaven is wide

'We've all been through this enough, to know that everything could turn on you like that', states Vig.

'We're natural pessimists',explains Erikson.

'I don't think any of us are ever content', agrees Marker.

'It's beyond our control', affirms Manson, 'but that's the way the whole world is - a lottery.'

Don't you just love Garbage's near-legendary, self-deprecating modesty? Despite almost convincing the NME's Sylvia Patterson that they might as well pack it all in, Garbage are, in fact, becoming more and more successful by the day, hijacking the mainstream charts the world over. No mean feat, especially in the agonisingly fashion-conscious UK, where they have managed to satisfy the 'indie elite', and appeal to everyone else - Radio 1 listeners, as well as people who know their shit. A testament to the fact that they have a firm grasp on what's what, having collectively accumulated a wealth of knowledge as to the way modern culture has ticked for the past 30 years.

That Garbage are switched on enough, young enough, capable enough and shot through with unbridled enthusiasm for their chosen medium, to step forward and express themselves with the kind of confidence born out of being sussed, points towards a career far beyond the shelf-life of most here-today-gone-tomorrow pop music artistes.

Even if they stood still and failed to develop their craft, we would still be comfortably (or should that be uncomfortably?) losing ourselves in their 'Twin Peaks-ian' world in ten years time, such is their lasting quality. But we know that won't happen. We know that, what with the creative doors that stand wide open before them, Garbage will continue to seek out new musical forms of giving vent to their unquiet souls.

So, although Garbage aren't by any stretch of the imagination, the most original band in the world, or the last word in rock-'n'roll, they have helped build a couple of much-needed bridges between one or two gaping chasms in Popular Music. They may well be a pointer towards the Music Of The Future, but they're also very much a Band Of Our Time, welding cutting-edge technology with infectious rhythms with catchy choons with attitude. Did someone call it 'popcore' out there? It's got a nice ring to it, I suppose, but in the end, it's just another label like 'punk rock' or 'grunge', and some bands transcend such trifles. Garbage are one of them.

You know the score, if only all bands were made this way...

Now the kind of info you've no doubt been waiting for...

20-odd Garbage facts

Kiss's Gene Simmons waggled that tongue at Manson at one American Garbage show. An honour indeed...

Covers : Garbage have been known to perform live, Vic Chestnut's song Supernatural, and they have recorded his Kick My Ass for the Sweet Relief II compilation. They've also covered The Jam's Butterfly Collector, which appears on Queer's CD2.

Shirley's all time favourite singer is Frank Sinatra.

Talking of covers, the Smurfs are reputedly recording a version of Stupid Girl called Stupid Smurf...oh dear...

At Manson's instigation, the boys in the band now have a penchant for garishly-painted fingernails, to, as she puts it, 'Get them in touch with their feminine side...'

Butch Vig was voted 'Most Creative' in the 1996 'Kerrang' Music Awards. Er, most creative what...?

In fact, Garbage wanted to sample a clarinet from a Sinatra song for Queer, but it would have proved too expensive.

Shirley has been known to refer to the guys in the band as 'my boys' or even, 'my babies'..

Shirley : 'The rest of the band have got bigger tits than me!'

The 'pig' in the foreground of Smashing Pumpkin's
Vieuphoria video is none other than Butch Vig. The video
also contains a Spinal Tap-esque 'interview' with him.

Garbage changed into kilts for the encore of the Glasgow
Barrowland leg of their first UK tour.

Episodes of TV shows Homicide and Roseanne used Garbage songs. And the band have contributed No 1 Crush to the Romeo & Juliet movie soundtrack.

Hundreds of kids were queuing up for Garbage's debut gig at a two-storey club in Minneapolis. Turns out they were there to see GWAR who were playing upstairs...

The pink feathers on the cover of Garbage are actually part of a
pink feather boa that Manson used to wrap around her mike stand on stage.

Shirley was voted second sexiest woman next to Alanis
Morissette in Much Music's 1996 poll.

Shirley's nickname is 'Charlie'

The name 'Butch' comes from the haircut Vig's father used to give him as a kid - a 'butch' cut is the same as a 'crew' cut.

Shirley's hubby is an artist/groundskeeper named Eddie.

Butch Vig used to be President of the Madison
Roxy Music Society at college. 'Nuff respect?
Spookily, given the above, Butch's real name is Bryan.

Satisfied?

DISCOGRAPHY

SINGLES

Vow/Vow (Torn Apart)
(March 20, 1995)
UK : (Discordant - through Mushroom - CORD001) 7-inch (limited 1000 metal sleeve)
US : (Almo Sounds, AMSDS - 88000, June 20) CD

Subhuman/No.1 Crush
(August 7, 1995)
UK : (Mushroom, SX1138) 7-inch (limited 3000 rubber sleeve), CD (D1138) includes Vow

Only Happy When It Rains/ Girl Don't Come / Sleep
(September 18, 1995)
UK : (Mushroom, SX1199) 7-inch (limited 5000 hologram sleeve), CD (D1199)
US : (Almo Sounds, AMSDS-89002, January 20) CD

Queer/Queer (Danny Saber Mix) (November 20, 1995)
UK : (Mushroom, SX1237) 7-inch (limited 11000 perspex sleeve sealed in bubblewrap), CD (D1237) includes Trip My Wire/Queer (The Very Queer Dub-Bin Mix)/Queer (The Most Beautiful Woman In Town Mix), CD (DX1237) includes Butterfly Collector/Queer (F.T.F.O.1. Mix)/Queer (Danny Saber Mix)

Stupid Girl/Dog New Tricks (Pal Mix) (March 10, 1996)
UK : (Mushroom, SX1271) 7-inch (limited 7500 cloth sleeves), CD1 (D1271) includes Driving Lesson/Stupid Girl (Red Snapper Mix). CD2 (DX1271) includes Alien Sex Fiend/Stupid Girl (Dreadzone Dub Version)/Stupid Girl (Dreadzone Vocal Mix)
US : (Almo Sounds, AMS12-88004) 12-inch (August 14) includes Stupid Girl (Tee's Freeze Club, Tees In-House Dub, Future Retro Mix, Danny Saber Mix and Shoegazer Mix)/Driving Lesson' CD (AMSDS-88004) includes Stupid Girl (Tee's Radio Mix)/Driving Lesson

Milk (Wicked Mix/Milk) (Tricky Remix)
UK : (Mushroom, SX1494) 7-inch (limited 15000 VideoGramTM sleeves) 12-inch (DJMILK1, October 28, 1996) limited 500 white label for one week through HMV. Remixes by Rabbit In The Moon including Milk (Got It Mix)/Milk (Butchered Vegas Mix/Milk (Utter Edit), 12-inch (DJMILK2, October 21) limited 500 white label for one week only. Remixes by Goldie including Milk (Completely Trashed Mix)/Milk (VIP Rufige Your Shit), 12-inch (DJMILK3, limited 500 white label for one week only. Remixed by

Massive Attack, including Milk(Trance Mix)/Milk(D Mix), CD 1 (D1494, November 11) includes Milk (The Wicked Mix Featuring Tricky)/Milk (Completely Trashed Mix)/Milk (Album Version)/Stupid Girl (Tees Radio Mix), CD2 (DX1494) includes Milk(The Wicked Mix Featuring Tricky/Milk (Classic Remix/ Milk (The Udder Remix/Stupid Girl (Danny Saber Remix)
US : (Almo Sounds, AMSDS-89007, November 19) CD includes Milk (The LP Version/ Milk (The Siren Mix/Milk (The Udder Mix)/Milk (The Wicked Mix)

ALBUMS

Garbage (October 2, 1995)
Supervixen/Queer/Only Happy When It Rains/As Heaven Is Wide/ Not My Idea/ A Stroke Of Luck/ Vow/ Stupid Girl/ Dog New Tricks/ My Lover's Box/ Fix Me Now/ Milk
UK : (Mushroom, LX31450) limited edition 6 x 7-inch colour coded singles with inserts, double LP (131450), CD (D31450)
US : (Almo Sounds, AMS2-80004), August 15, 1995, double LP

BIBLIOGRAPHY

Raw # 186
(Valerie Potter)
Raw 13/3/96
(Cathi Unsworth)
Record Collector #209
(Andy Davis)
Retroactive Baggage
(Tim Sismey)
Features March 1997
(Mike Gee)
Feminism Amplified
(Kim France)
Details November 1995
Rolling Stone 17/10/96
(Jancee Dunn)
i-d, June 1996
(Frank Broughton)
Addicted To Noise
(Gil Kaufman)
NME 6/5/95
(Simon Williams)
NME 12/8/95
(Amy Raphael)
NME 19/10/96
NME 16/3/97
(Sylvia Patterson)
Brum Beat, Dec 96/Jan 97
(Max)
Hot Press 1996
Volume # 12
(Anne Scanlon)
Guitar Vol. 6, No 6
(Danny Eccleston)
Arena June 1996
(Sean Langan)
Select June 1996
(Gina Morris)
Select (Caspar Smith)
Melody Maker 18/3/95
(Dave Simpson)
Melody Maker 8/6/96
(Dave Bennun)
Goldmine #398 (Jim Berkenstadt)
Creem October 1993
(Barry Egan)
Vox October 1995
(Steve Malins)

THANKS TO :
(in no particular order!)
Rob from Pomona, Shannon from SOS, Scott, Juanita, Maria from HMV, Simon from Flipside, Sean Redmond, Christine Gillian, Steve from Brum Beat, and web sites:
http://ps.cus.umist.ac.uk.
htpp://www.csv.warwick.ac.uk
htpp://www.thei.aust.comm.
htpp://www.execpc.com.
htpp//www.addict.com.
htpp://www.garbage.net
htpp://www.geffen.com.
htpp://users.hol.
htpp://www.addict.com.
htpp://www.chem.surrey.ac.u k
htpp://www.enter.net

Lyrics copyright of:
Vibecrusher Music/Irving Music, Inc, BMI/Deadarm Music, ASCAP

Official Garbage fan club:
Garbage Zone, 300 Queen Anne Avenue, N. Suite 332, Seattle, WA, 98109, USA